كانَتْ نِيتا تَلْعَبُ بالكُرَة مع روكي. " إمسك! " صَرَخَتْ.
فَقَفَزَ روكي لكنَّهُ أَخْطَأَ، ثُمَّ ركَضَ وَراءَ الكرة خارِجَ
الحديقَةِ إلى الطريق. " قِفْ! روكي! قِفْ! " صَرَخَتْ نيتا.
إِنشَغَلَتْ تُحَاوِلُ أَنْ تُمسِكَ بروكي فَلَمْ تَرَ...

Nita was playing ball with Rocky. "Catch!" she shouted. Rocky jumped,
missed and ran after the ball, out of the park and into the road.
"STOP! ROCKY! STOP!" Nita shouted. She was so busy trying to catch
Rocky that she didn't see …

...السيارة.

the CAR.

دَعَسَ السائِقُ على الفَرَامِلْ بقوةٍ. زي ي ي!! لكِنْ دونَ جَدْوى!
بوم! ضَرَبَت السيارةُ نِيتا، فوَقَعَت نِيتا على الأرضِ بِخَبطةٍ مُرْعِبَةٍ.

The driver slammed on the brakes. SCREECH! But it was too late! THUD!
The car hit Nita and she fell to the ground with a sickening CRUNCH.

" نيتا! " صَرَخَت أُمُّها. " أُطلبوا سيَّارةَ الإِسْعَافِ! " قَالَت صَارِخَةً.

ثُمَّ حَضَنَت نيتا وأَخَذَت تُمَلِّسُ شَعْرَهَا.

تَلْفَنَ السَائِقُ لِسيَّارَةِ الإِسعَافِ.

" ماما سَاقي تُوجِعُني، " بكَتْ نيتا والدُموعُ تَتَدَحْرَجُ على وَجْهِهَا.

" أَنا أَعْلَمُ أَنَّها تُوجِعُكِ، لَكِنْ لا تَتَحَرَكي، " قَالَت الأُمُّ.

" الإِسعَافُ على طَرِيقهِ الينا. "

"NITA!" Ma screamed. "Someone call an ambulance!" she shouted, stroking Nita's hair and holding her.
The driver dialled for an ambulance.
"Ma, my leg hurts," cried Nita, big tears rolling down her face.
"I know it hurts, but try not to move," said Ma. "Help will be here soon."

وَصَلَت سيَّارةُ الإِسْعَاف وحضَرَ رَجُلا إِسْعَاف ومعهُمَا حَمَّالة.

" مرحباً، أَنا جون.إِنَّ سَاقَك مُتَوَرِّمَةٌ جداً. لَعَلَّها مكسورة. "

ثُمَّ قَالَ لهَا: " سأضَعُ هاتيْنِ الخَشبتين عَليهَا لتُمْسكَاهَا. "

شَدَّتْ نيتا على شفَتيهَا. كَانت رِجْلُهَا تُوجعُهَا جداً.

قَالَ جون: " أَنْت فَتاةٌ شجَاعَةٌ. " ثُمَّ حملَهَا برِفقٍ على
الحَمَّالةِ إِلى سيَّارَةِ الإِسعَافِ. صَعِدَتْ أُمُّهَا في السيارةِ أَيضاً.

The ambulance arrived and two paramedics came with a stretcher.
"Hello, I'm John. Your leg's very swollen. It might be broken," he said.
"I'm just going to put these splints on to stop it from moving."
Nita bit her lip. The leg was really hurting.
"You're a brave girl," he said, carrying her gently on the stretcher to
the ambulance. Ma climbed in too.

إِستَلْقَت نِيتا على الحَمَّالة وتَمَسَّكَتْ بأُمِها جيداً، بينَمَا أَسرَعَت سيارَةُ الإِسْعَاف في الطُرُقاتِ - صَفَّارَتُهَا تُصَفِرُ بِحِدَّةٍ وأنَوارُها تُطْفِئُ وتَضِيءُ - إِلى أن وصلَتْ إِلى المُستَشفَى.

Nita lay on the stretcher holding tight to Ma, while the ambulance raced through the streets – siren wailing, lights flashing – all the way to the hospital.

كَانَ عِندَ المَدخَلِ أُنَاسٌ في كلِّ مكانٍ. فَزِعَت نِيتا فَزَعاً شَدِيداً.

" ماذا حَلَّ بِكِ؟ " سَأَلَتْهَا مُمَرِضَةٌ لَطِيفَةٌ.

" ضَرَبتِني سَيَارةٌ وسَاقي تُؤْلِمُني كَثيراً، " أَجابَتْ نيتا مُحاوِلَةً كَبْتَ دُموعِهَا.

قَالت المُمَرِضَةُ: " سَنُعطيكِ مُسكِّناً للوَجَعِ إلى أن يَرَاكِ الطَبيبُ.

أَمَّا الآن، فَيَجبُ أن أَفحصَ حَرَارتَكِ وآخُذَ بَعضَ الدَّمِ.

لَنْ تَشعُرِينَ إلاَّ بوكْزَةٍ خَفيفةٍ. "

At the entrance there were people everywhere. Nita was feeling very scared.
"Oh dear, what's happened to you?" asked a friendly nurse.
"A car hit me and my leg really hurts," said Nita, blinking back the tears.
"We'll give you something for the pain, as soon as the doctor has had a look,"
he told her. "Now I've got to check your temperature and take some blood.
You'll just feel a little jab."

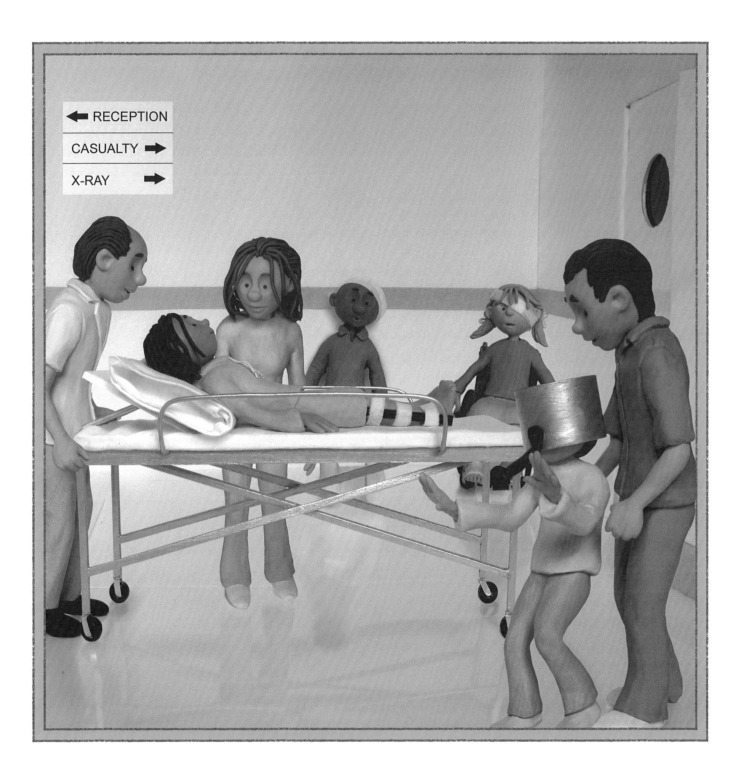

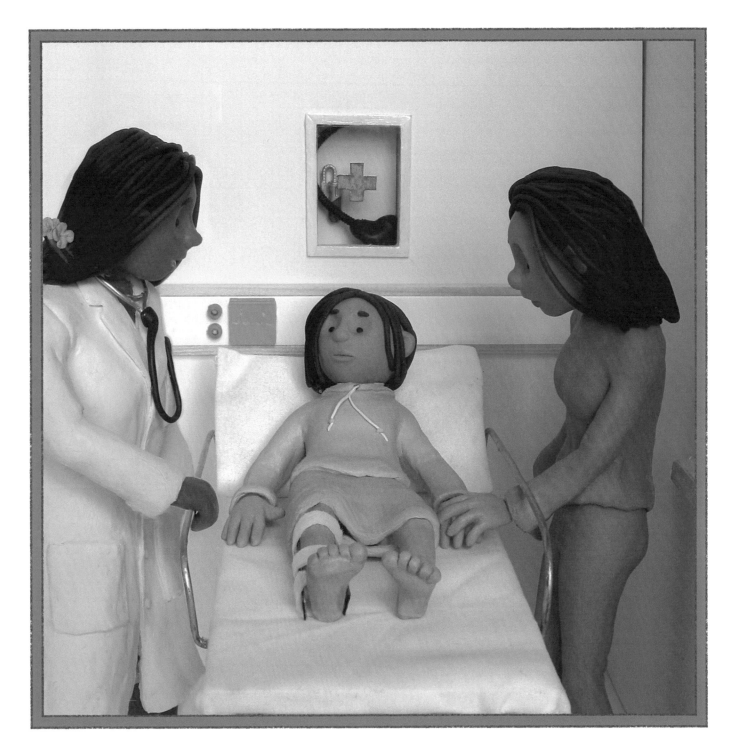

ثُمَّ جَاءَتِ الطَبيبَةُ وقَالت: " مَرْحَباً يا نِيتا. آهْ... كيفَ حصلَ هذا؟! "

" ضَربَتْني سيَارةٌ. سَاقِي تُؤْلمُني جداً، " بكَتْ نيتا.

" سَأُعْطيكِ مُسكِّناً لإيقَافِ الوجعِ. أريني سَاقَكِ الآن، " قَالتِ الطبيبةُ.

" هُمْ... يَبْدو أَنها مكسَورَةٌ. يُلزِمُنَا صُورَةٌ بالأَشِعةِ كي نَتأَكَّدَ مِن هذا. "

Next came the doctor. "Hello Nita," she said. "Ooh, how did that happen?"
"A car hit me. My leg really hurts," sobbed Nita.
"I'll give you something to stop the pain. Now let's have a look at your leg," said the doctor. "Hmm, it seems broken. We'll need an x-ray to take a closer look."

نَقَلَ حَمَّالٌ لَطيفٌ نيتا إلى قِسمِ الأَشِعَةِ حَيثُ كانَ أَشخاصٌ كَثيرونَ يَنتظِرونَ. أَخيراً جَاءَ دَورُ نيتا. "مَرحباً نِيتا،" قَالت أَخصَائِيَةُ التَصويرِ بالأَشِعَةِ. "سآخُذُ صورةً لِدَاخِل سَاقِك بهذهِ الآلةِ. لا تَقلَقي هَذا لَنْ يُؤلِمَك. يَجبْ أَن لا تَتَحَرَّكي أَبداً عِندَمَا أَقومُ بِأَخذِ الصورَةِ."

هَزَّت نِيتا بِرَأْسِهَا.

A friendly porter wheeled Nita to the x-ray department where lots of people were waiting.
At last it was Nita's turn. "Hello Nita," said the radiographer. "I'm going to take a picture of the inside of your leg with this machine," she said pointing to the x-ray machine. "Don't worry, it won't hurt. You just have to keep very still while I take the x-ray."
Nita nodded.

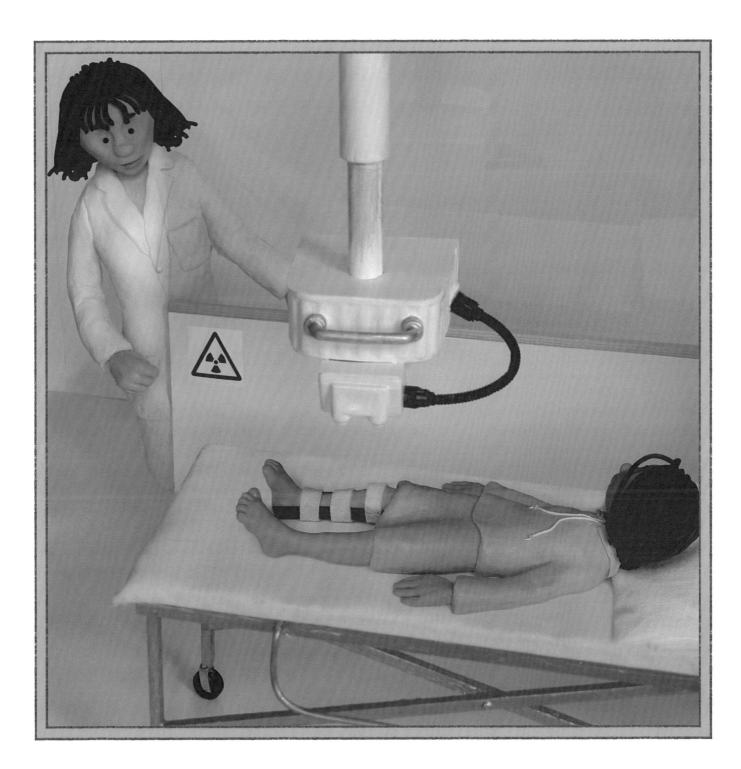

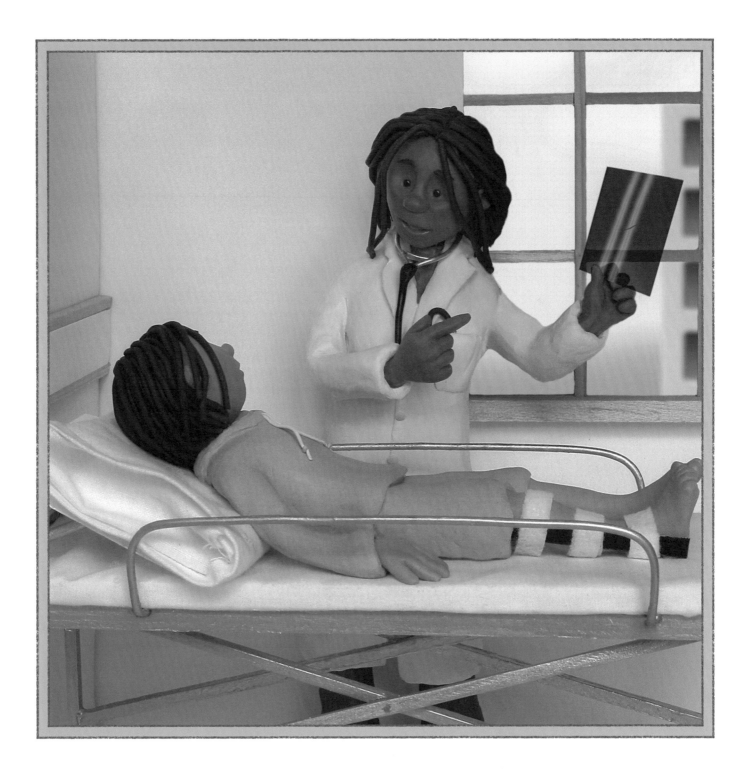

بَعْدَ قليلٍ حَضَرتِ الطبيبةُ حامِلَةً صُورَةَ الأَشِعَةِ السينِيَّةِ.

رَفَعَتْهَا إلى الأَعْلَى فرَأَتْ نيتَا العَظْمَةَ داخلَ ساقِهَا!

" هَذا مَا كُنْتُ أَظُنُّهُ، " قَالَت الطبيبَة.

" إنَّ ساقَكِ مكْسُورَةٌ. يَجِبُ أَنْ نُعيدَ العَظْمَةَ إِلى مَكَانِهَا ثُمَّ نُجَبِّرَهَا. التَجْبِيرُ سَيُثَبّتُ العَظْمَةَ في مَكَانِهَا كَيْ تَصِحَّ.

أَمَّا الآن فَسَاقُكِ مُتَورِمَةٌ جِداً. يَجِب أَن تَبيتي هذه اللَيلَةُ هُنَا. "

A little later the doctor came with the x-ray. She held it up and Nita could see the bone right inside her leg!
"It's as I thought," said the doctor. "Your leg is broken. We'll need to set it and then put on a cast. That'll hold it in place so that the bone can mend. But at the moment your leg is too swollen. You'll have to stay overnight."

نَقَلَ الحَمَّالُ نِيتا إِلى جِناحِ الأَوْلادِ. "مَرحباً نِيتا، إِسمي روز. أَنا مُمَرِضَتُكِ الخاصَةُ. سَأَهتَمُّ بِكِ. لَقَدْ جِئْتِ في الوقْتِ المُنَاسِبِ،" قالتْ مُبْتَسِمَةً.

" لِمَاذَا؟ " سَأَلَتْ نِيتا.

" لأَنَّهُ وَقْتُ العَشاءِ. سَأَضَعُكِ في السَرِيرِ ثُمَّ أُعطِيكِ طَعامَكِ. " وَضَعَتِ المُمَرِضَةُ روز ثَلجاً حَولَ سَاقِ نِيتا ثُمَّ أَعْطَتْهَا مِخَدَّةً إِضَافِيةً لا لِرَأْسِهَا... بَل لِسَاقِهَا.

The porter wheeled Nita to the children's ward. "Hello Nita. My name's Rose and I'm your special nurse. I'll be looking after you. You've come just at the right time," she smiled.
"Why?" asked Nita.
"Because it's dinner time. We'll pop you into bed and then you can have some food."
Nurse Rose put some ice around Nita's leg and gave her an extra pillow, not for her head… but for her leg.

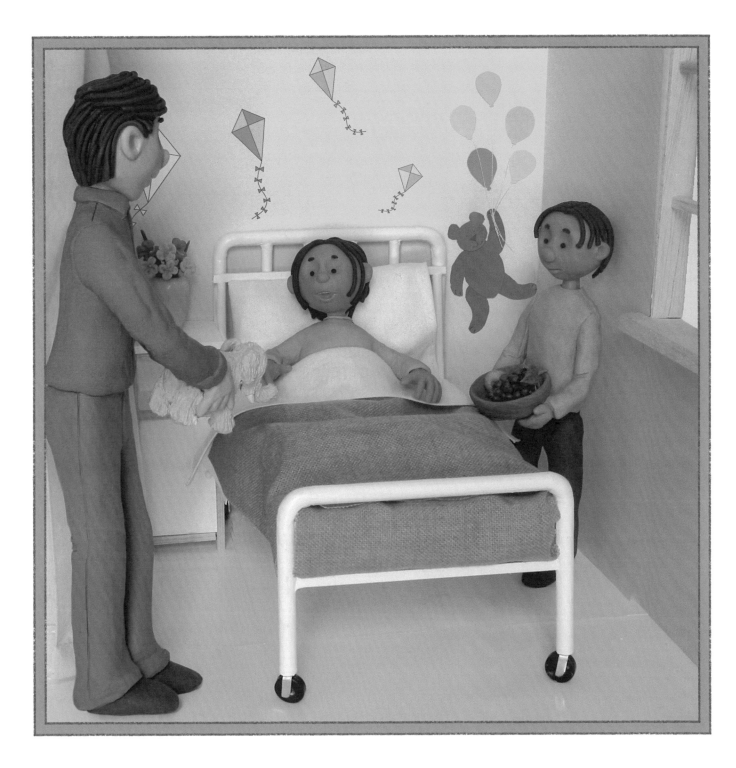

بَعْدَ العَشَاءِ، وَصَلَ أَبُوهَا وَأَخُوها جاي. ضَمَّهَا أَبُوهَا إِلى صَدرِهِ و أَعْطَاهَا لُعبَتَهَا المُفَضلَة.

" هَل يُمْكِنُ أَن أَرى سَاقَكِ؟ " سَأَلَ جاي. " آخْ! هَذا شَنيعٌ. هَل تُوجِعُكِ؟ " " كَثيراً، " أَجابَتْ نِيتا. " لَكِنَهُم أَعْطُوني مُسَكِّناً لِلوجَع. "

أَخَذَت المُمَرِّضَةُ روز حَرَارَةَ نِيتا مَرَّةَ ثَانية. ثُمَّ قَالَت: " حَلَّ وَقْتُ النومِ. يَجبُ أَن يَذْهَبَ أَبوكِ وأَخوكِ لَكِنَّ أُمَّكِ يُمكِنُ أَن تَبقَى...كُلَّ اللَيلِ. "

After dinner Dad and Jay arrived. Dad gave her a big hug and her favourite toy.
"Let's see your leg?" asked Jay. "Ugh! It's horrible. Does it hurt?"
"Lots," said Nita, "but they gave me pain-killers."
Nurse Rose took Nita's temperature again. "Time to sleep now," she said.
"Dad and your brother will have to go but Ma can stay... all night."

في الصَّباحِ البَاكِرِ فَحَصَتِ الطَّبِيبَةُ سَاقَ نِيتا وقَالَت: " هَذا أَحسَنُ بِكَثيرٍ. أَظُنُّ أَنَهُ حَلَّ وَقْتُ تجبيرُهَا. "

" ماذا يَعني هَذا؟ " سَأَلَتْ نِيتا.

" سَنُعطيكِ بِنجاً لِيُنَيِّمَكِ. ثُمَّ نَدْفَعُ العَظمَةَ إِلى مكَانِهَا الصَحِيحِ ونُمْسِكُهَا بِقَالِبِ جِبْسْ. لا تَقْلَقِي، لَن تَشْعُرِي بِشيءٍ، " قَالَتِ الطَّبيبَةُ.

Early next morning the doctor checked Nita's leg. "Well that looks much better," she said. "I think it's ready to be set."

"What does that mean?" asked Nita.

"We're going to give you an anaesthetic to make you sleep. Then we'll push the bone back in the right position and hold it in place with a cast. Don't worry, you won't feel a thing," said the doctor.

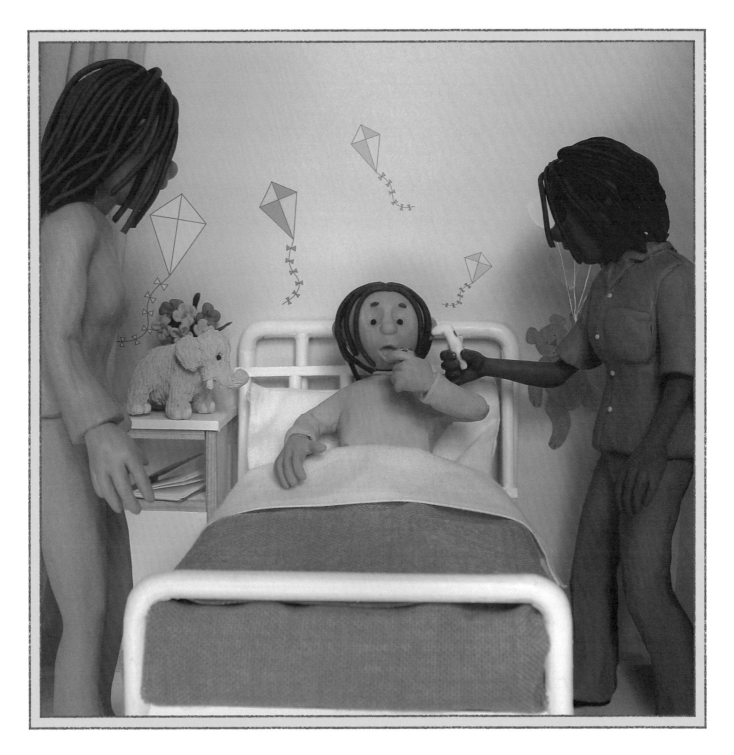

شَعَرَت نيتا أَنَها نَامَت أُسبُوعاً كَامِلاً فَسأَلَت: " مَامَا كَم نِمتُ مِنَ الوَقْتِ؟ "

" فقطْ سَاعَةً، " إِبتَسَمَت الأُمُّ.

" مرحباً نيتا، " قَالَتِ المُمَرِضَةُ روز . " إِني مَسرورَةٌ أَنَّكِ إِستَيْقَظتِ . كَيفَ سَاقُكِ؟ "

" إِنَهَا جَيِّدَة، لَكِني أَحِسُّ بِأَنَها ثَقِيلَةً ويَابِسةً، " قَالت نيتا .

" هَل يُمكِنُني أَن آكُلَ شيئاً؟ "

" نَعَم، حَانَ وَقْتُ الغذَاءِ، " قَالَت روز .

Nita felt like she'd been asleep for a whole week. "How long have I been sleeping, Ma?" she asked.
"Only about an hour," smiled Ma.
"Hello Nita," said Nurse Rose. "Good to see you've woken up. How's the leg?"
"OK, but it feels so heavy and stiff," said Nita. "Can I have something to eat?"
"Yes, it'll be lunchtime soon," said Rose.

عِندَ الظُهرِ شَعَرَت نِيتا بِالتَحَسُّنِ. وضَعَتْها المُمَرِضةُ روز في كُرسِّيٍ بِدَواليبَ لِكَيّ تجتَمِعَ بِسَائِرِ الأَولاد.

" مَاذا جَرَى لَكِ؟ " سَأَلَ أَحَدُ الأَولاد.

" إِنكَسَرتُ سَاقي، " قَالَت نِيتا. "وأَنْتَ؟ "

" أُجْرِيَتُ عَمَلِيَّةٌ جِرَاحِيَّةٌ لِأُذُني، " أجابَ الوَلَدُ.

By lunchtime Nita was feeling much better. Nurse Rose put her in a wheelchair so that she could join the other children.
"What happened to you?" asked a boy.
"Broke my leg," said Nita. "And you?"
"I had an operation on my ears," said the boy.

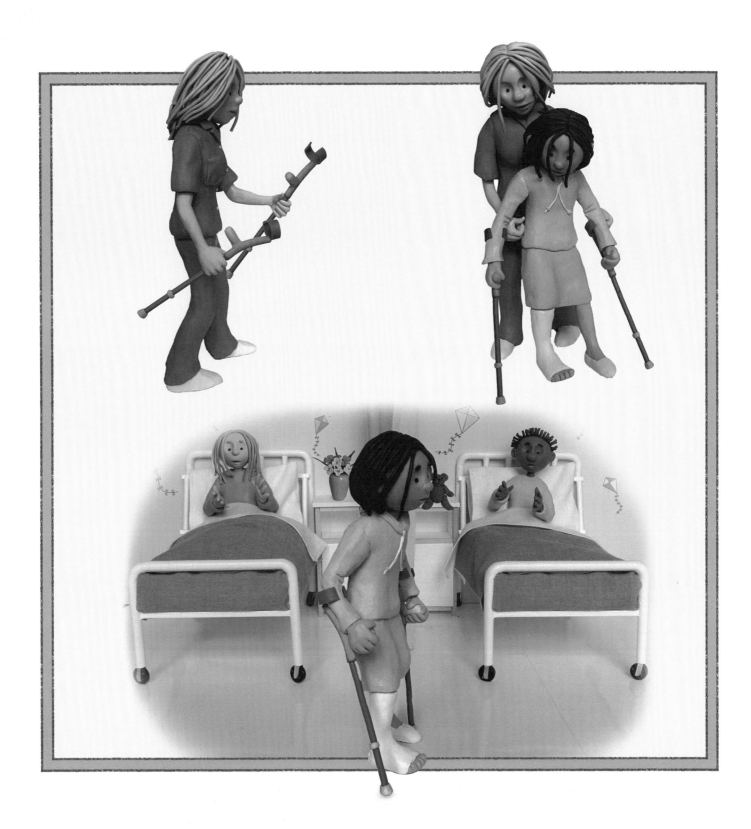

بعدَ الظُّهرِ جَاءَت أَخِصَائِيَّةُ التَدْليكِ بِعَكَّازَيْنِ وقالت: " خُذِي يا نيتا. هذه سَتُسَاعِدُكِ عَلى المَشيِ. "

بِعَرْجَةٍ وهَزَّةٍ ودَفْعَةٍ ومَسْكَةٍ، ما لبثت أَنْ مَشَتْ نيتا في جِنَاحِ الأَولادِ.

" عظيمٌ! " قَالت الأَخِصَائِيَّةُ: " أَظُنُّ أَنَكِ مُسْتَعِدَةٌ لِلْعَودَةِ إِلى البَيتِ. سَأَطْلُبُ مِنَ الطَبِيبِ أَن يَرَاكِ. "

In the afternoon the physiotherapist came with some crutches. "Here you are Nita. These will help you to get around," she said.
Hobbling and wobbling, pushing and holding, Nita was soon walking around the ward.
"Well done," said the physiotherapist. "I think you're ready to go home. I'll get the doctor to see you."

في المَساءِ، جَاءَ البَابا والمَاما وجاي وروكي لإرجَاعٍ نِيتا إِلى البَيتِ.

" عَظِيم! " قَالَ جاي عِنْدَمَا رَأَى القَالبَ.

" هَل يُمكِنُني أن أَرْسُمَ عَلَيهِ؟ "

" لَيسَ الآنَ! عِندَمَا نَصِلُ إِلى البَيتِ، " قَالَتْ نِيتا.

لَعَلَّ قَالِبَ الجبسِ هَذا لَن يَكونَ سَيِّئاً فِيمَا بَعْد.

That evening Ma, Dad, Jay and Rocky came to collect Nita.
"Cool," said Jay seeing Nita's cast. "Can I draw on it?"
"Not now! When we get home," said Nita. Maybe having a
cast wasn't going to be so bad.